MR.PERFECT

by Roger Hargreaves

It was a perfect summer's day.

And on this perfect summer's day,
Mr Perfect was looking more perfect
than usual.

He didn't have a hair out of place.

Mr Perfect lived in Tiptop Cottage.

And on this perfect summer's day,
his house was also looking even more
perfect than usual.

Not a curtain out of place.

I suppose you're wondering why
Tiptop Cottage was looking so perfect.

I shall tell you.

It was Mr Perfect's birthday,
and he was going to have a party.

There was a knock at the door.
"Perfect!" cried Mr Perfect.

"How very kind of you," he said, when he saw that all his guests had brought wonderful-looking presents. "Please do come in and if no one minds, we'll open the presents later."

Nobody minded in the least.

Well almost nobody.

"WHAT'S THAT?" roared Mr Uppity.

"I don't have any time to waste, you know!
You'd better make sure we
don't get bored today!"

Do you think this upset Mr Perfect?

Of course not.

Mr Perfect had perfect manners,
unlike rude Mr Uppity.

"Oh no, my dear Mr Uppity,
we shan't be bored today," he replied.
"First of all we shall dance."

And everybody danced.

Even Mr Uppity.

But although he danced, Mr Uppity couldn't manage a smile.

Unfortunately, Mr Clumsy,
being his usual clumsy self,
broke a pile of plates.

Do you think this upset Mr Perfect?

Not at all.

"Don't worry, Mr Clumsy," said Mr Perfect.

And, being the perfect person he was,
and not in the least bit clumsy,
he produced a whole lot more plates ...

... made of cardboard!

Then, he brought in a cake.

It was huge.

It looked wonderful.

It smelt terrific.

And ...

Mr Greedy thought it tasted delicious.

He gobbled up the whole cake
in three seconds flat!

There wasn't a crumb left for anybody else!

Do you think this upset Mr Perfect?

Not in the least.

Being perfect, he had already guessed
what would happen.

Quickly, he brought out lots of small cakes.

There were plenty for everybody.

Even Mr Perfect.

But as he was not greedy, he only ate one.

One cake was just perfect for him.

Once everything had been eaten,
Mr Perfect opened his presents.

He said as many thank-yous as
there were presents.

Well, not quite.

"What about my present?" cried Mr Mean.

Mr Mean's parcel was so small that
Mr Perfect had not seen it!

Mr Perfect opened the tiny parcel,
wrapped in newspaper.

"Oh, Mr Mean," said Mr Perfect.
"You've given me a lump of coal.
How kind of you!
It's delightful!"

"If I'd known, I'd only have given him
half a lump," grumbled Mr Mean.

"THAT'S IT! I've had enough!"
cried Mr Uppity, suddenly.

"I'm fed up with you, Mr Perfect. And do you
know why? I'll tell you! I have discovered
that there is a most enormous,unbearable,
exasperating fault with you."

"Would you be so kind as to tell me what
that might be?" asked Mr Perfect,
as politely as ever.

"Don't you understand?" cried Mr Uppity.
"Your fault is ...

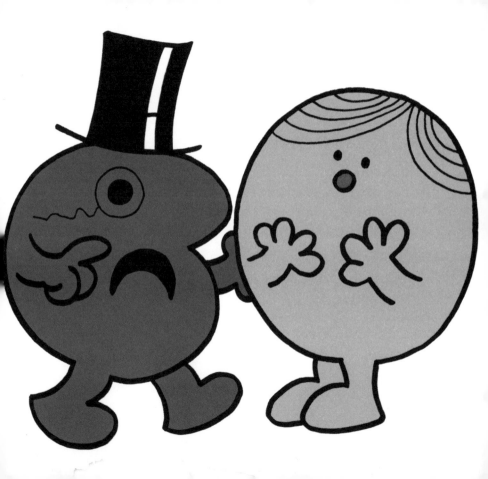

... that you have NO faults!"

Only need a few Mr. Men or Little Miss to complete your set? You can order any of the titles on the back of the books from our Mr. Men order line on 0870 787 1724. Orders should be delivered between 5 and 7 working days.

— TO BE COMPLETED BY AN ADULT —

To apply for any of these great offers, ask an adult to complete the details below and send this whole page with the appropriate payment and tokens, to: MR. MEN CLASSIC OFFER, PO BOX 715, HORSHAM RH12 5WG

☐ Please send me a giant-sized double-sided collectors' poster.

AND ☐ I enclose 6 tokens and have taped a £1 coin to the other side of this page.

☐ Please send me ☐ Mr. Men Library case(s) and/or ☐ Little Miss library case(s) at £5.99 each inc P&P

☐ I enclose a cheque/postal order payable to Egmont UK Limited for £...................

OR ☐ Please debit my MasterCard / Visa / Maestro / Delta account (delete as appropriate) for £...................

Card no. ☐☐☐☐ ☐☐☐☐ ☐☐☐☐ ☐☐☐☐ ☐☐☐☐   Security code ☐☐☐

Issue no. (if available) ☐   Start Date ☐☐/☐☐/☐☐   Expiry Date ☐☐/☐☐/☐☐

Fan's name: ....   Date of birth: ....

Address: ....

....

....   Postcode: ....

Name of parent / guardian: ....

Email for parent / guardian: ....

Signature of parent / guardian: ....

Please allow 28 days for delivery. Offer is only available while stocks last. We reserve the right to change the terms of this offer at any time and we offer a 14 day money back guarantee. This does not affect your statutory rights. Offers apply to UK only.

☐ We may occasionally wish to send you information about other Egmont children's books. If you would rather we didn't, please tick this box.

Ref: MRM 001

cut along the dotted line and return this whole page

Fantastic offers for Mr. Men fans!

Collect all your Mr. Men or Little Miss books in these superb durable collectors' cases!

Only £5.99 inc. postage and packing, these wipe-clean, hard-wearing cases will give all your Mr. Men or Little Miss books a beautiful new home!

Keep track of your collection with this giant-sized double-sided Mr. Men and Little Miss Collectors' poster.

Collect 6 tokens and we will send you a brilliant giant-sized double-sided collectors' poster! Simply tape a £1 coin to cover postage and packaging in the space provided and fill out the form overleaf.

STICK £1 COIN HERE (for poster only)

Cut along the dotted line and return this whole page